PUFFIN BOOKS
Published by the Penguin Group
Penguin Group (NZ), 67 Apollo Drive, Rosedale,
Auckland 0632, New Zealand (a division of Pearson New Zealand Ltd)
Penguin Group (USA) Inc., 375 Hudson Street,
New York, New York 10014, USA
Penguin Group (Canada), 90 Eglinton Avenue East, Suite 700, Toronto,
Ontario, M4P 2Y3, Canada (a division of Pearson Penguin Canada Inc.)
Penguin Books Ltd, 80 Strand, London, WC2R 0RL, England
Penguin Ireland, 25 St Stephen's Green,
Dublin 2, Ireland (a division of Penguin Books Ltd)
Penguin Group (Australia), 250 Camberwell Road, Camberwell,
Victoria 3124, Australia (a division of Pearson Australia Group Pty Ltd)
Penguin Books India Pvt Ltd, 11, Community Centre,
Panchsheel Park, New Delhi – 110 017, India
Penguin Books (South Africa) (Pty) Ltd, Block D, Rosebank Office Park,
181 Jan Smuts Avenue, Parktown North, Gauteng 2193, South Africa

Penguin Books Ltd, Registered Offices: 80 Strand, London, WC2R 0RL, England

Published by Puffin Books, 2012
10 9 8 7 6 5 4 3 2 1

Designed and typeset by Vida & Luke Kelly Design
Text by Margaret Mahy
Illustrations by Gavin Bishop
Prepress by Image Centre, Ltd
Printed in China by South China Printing Company

ISBN 978-0-143-50557-0

A catalogue record for this book is available
from the National Library of New Zealand.

www.penguin.co.nz

ROYAL NEW ZEALAND
**FOUNDATION OF
THE BLIND**
TE TUĀPAPA O TE HUNGA KĀPŌ O AOTEAROA

Footsteps through the Fog

Written by Margaret Mahy

Illustrated by Gavin Bishop

PUFFIN BOOKS

'*T*he day is clouding over. There's fog on the harbour,' said Mrs Patton. 'You kids had better run down to the beach and get a bit of exercise before it starts to rain.'

There were five kids: Charlie and Max, the twin brothers; Ivy (the big girl), Wendy (the little girl) and Anthea, who was middle sized.

'Take care of Anthea,' said Mrs Patton. 'Don't let her fall over.'

'She should stay at home,' said Ivy. 'She won't be able to see the sea.'

'I've been down there lots of times,' said Anthea. 'I can't see the sea, but I can smell it, and I can hear it. And I can feel the sand. And you fall over just as much as I do.'

'I'll take your hand,' said Wendy. 'I can guide you.'

'You guide me, and I'll guide you,' said Anthea. 'My cane's pretty useful. And anyway, I listen hard. I reckon I listen harder than anyone else.'

They set off past a row of letterboxes and then turned into a road with tall trees growing on either side of it.

'Listen to the trees whispering secrets to each other,' said Anthea.

'You're making up stories again,' said Ivy.

'I like her stories,' said Wendy.

They went past the house with the rose garden in front of it, then past the long hedge of lavender bushes and then down stony steps to the place they called 'the star' because two roads crossed and a third road came down from the hills and joined in. You could go in any direction . . . backwards, forwards, up and down. But the sea was murmuring down below them so they chose the downhill road and made for the beach.

They passed the little cake-and-bread shop, and then the last house of all. Mrs Morrison was busy in her kitchen. She waved to them as they went by and they waved back.

'What are you doing?' asked Anthea.

'Waving to Mrs Morrison!' said Charlie. Anthea waved too.

'Hey! Be careful with that cane!' shouted Ivy. 'You nearly hit me with it.'

They went on down, under more tall trees (all muttering to each other in rustle-rustle language), then over the old bridge, down five more steps and, suddenly, there they were on the beach.

Waves were breaking on the sand, running up towards them, then sighing as they ran backwards again. Seagulls called to one another, warning each other that people were coming down to the beach. Charlie and Max shouted and ran off along the sand.

'There's a log here,' Ivy said to Anthea. 'The boys have run away and Wendy's already wandering. You can sit here while I go after them.'

Anthea sat on the log and sniffed the salt-and-seaweed smell. She listened to the sea sound, which was like the day's slow heartbeat.

Behind her she could hear the sound of the busy creek running under the old bridge. She sat there, listening to the two different water sounds . . . the boom of the sea on the sand and the chatter of the creek tumbling down to meet the sea. After a while she bent down to touch the sand and sifted it through her fingers. And then she stood up and walked towards those waves.

She could tell what was in front of her by touching the sand with her cane. Sand and shells. More sand and shells. A plastic bag perhaps. Sand and shells again. Something she could not be sure of. What's that? She bent over and touched what her cane had discovered. An old shoe soggy with sea water. Far down the beach she could hear her brothers and sisters shouting as they chased one another. A faint breeze blew in on her. It was almost as if the sea was breathing her a secret message.

'It's getting cold,' she thought. And, as she thought this, a little wave washed in over her feet then ran back into the sea, just as if it were ashamed of itself. Time to go back up the beach once more.

It was hard for Anthea to find the exact log she had been sitting on. She was still looking for it when she heard footsteps galloping towards her. Her brothers and sisters were coming back . . . quickly! Quickly!

'Fog,' Ivy was shouting. 'One of those fogs.'

'It's rolling in on us,' said Wendy. 'It wasn't there, and then, suddenly, it was.'

'Hey!' said Charlie. 'We'd better get home. I can hardly see the bridge. Well, I can't see it any more.'

'It was there just a moment ago and now it's gone,' cried Max. 'The fog's just swallowed the world.'

'That's OK,' said Anthea.
'I know where the bridge is.
I can hear it.'
	'Hear it?' said Ivy. 'How
can you hear a bridge?'
	'The water running
underneath it,' Anthea
explained. 'It's over there.'
She pointed with her cane.
	'I can hear it a bit,' said Charlie. 'But the fog's getting
so thick.'
	'So thick so suddenly!' said Wendy.
	'I'll show you the way,' said Anthea. 'When we come to the
bridge we'll be able to get back onto the road.'

They moved up over the damp sand onto the dry sand. The voice of the creek grew louder and louder.

'The bridge,' Anthea said. 'It must be just up here.' She waved her cane and it hit hard wood. 'There it is. Up three big steps and two little ones and onto it.'

Slowly, slowly they felt their way up the steps and over the bridge.

'We're on the road,' said Anthea. 'Now we go up hill for
a bit. Listen to the trees whispering to one another. And I can
smell the dinner Mrs Morrison was cooking. And I can smell
the bread and cake in that baker's shop. I'm good at smelling
things.'

'I can see lights,' said Ivy. 'They look so funny in the fog –
just as if the light and the fog are melting into one another.'

They went past the shops. Wendy sniffed at the baking smell as they went by the baker's shop. But they left the misty shop lights behind them and suddenly it seemed they were swimming through a sort of grey soup. This fog was a very thick fog . . . the thickest they could ever remember.

'We might be pushing our way into a different world,' said Max.

'I don't want to,' said Wendy, sounding rather frightened. 'I like our world best. I just want to get home.'

'We will get home,' said Anthea. 'We're almost at that street-star. Well, we are at the star. This way!'

'How do you know which way?' asked Charlie.

'Because I can smell the lavender hedge up there,' said Anthea. 'I can't see, but I can smell. I've had a lot of practice at smelling things. Be careful not to fall into a ditch. Hold onto me, Ivy. And you boys hold onto Ivy. And Wendy, you take my free hand. Here is the first step. Here are the stairs. Here we go. There are twenty-three steps. Count them.'

'How do you know there are twenty-three?' asked Charlie.

'Four . . . five . . . six . . .' counted Anthea. 'Because I'm used to counting steps. Twenty-three uphill here and eight down to our gate.'

'We're counting our way home,' said Max. 'Twenty, twenty-one, twenty-two, twenty-three!'

'I can smell that lavender now,' said Wendy.

'We're smelling our way home,' said Charlie.

Anthea swung her cane right and left.

'We're on the edge of the road,' she told them. 'The gravel's thick just here. But we're leaving the lavender behind us. I'm beginning to smell the roses.'

'How do we know where we are now?' asked Ivy a moment later. 'There's nothing to smell any more.'

'Listen!' said Anthea. 'Listen to the trees. We're going along beside them and we can hear them talking to each other. Stand still and listen.'

There they stood while the thick fog wrapped itself around them. Up over their heads they could hear a faint, high-up rustling. Over to one side of them that rustling went on and on.

'There's no wind,' said Ivy. 'How can the trees rustle?'

'There's no real wind,' agreed Anthea, 'but the air is moving just a little. And when it moves the leaves move too. This way.'

She held her cane sideways. Suddenly there was a clanging noise.

'That's the letterbox at the corner,' she said. 'Turn here. Follow me.'

Slowly, slowly they trailed through the thick fog. Anthea first, with Wendy holding her hand and walking half a step behind her, Ivy holding the back of Wendy's jersey, Max holding Ivy's jacket and Charlie hooking his fingers at the back of Max's belt.

'We're like a fog crocodile,' said Max.

'Step by step! Step by step!' said Charlie.

Anthea's cane hit something that made a hollow wooden sound.

'That's Mrs Wooten's letter box,' said Anthea. 'Nearly home now.'

Then, somewhere ahead of them,
a voice called out.

'You kids! Are you there?'

'Mum!' shouted Wendy. 'Nearly
home. Anthea rescued us.'

And in a moment they suddenly
saw a light.

'I was just coming out to look for you,'
their mother was saying.

'Anthea rescued us by smelling and listening,' Wendy said.

'She smelt her way home,' said Max.

'She knows what letterboxes sound like,' said Charlie.

'She was great,' said Ivy.

'When you can't see, listening and smelling tell you what's going on,' said Anthea. 'It's easy to get lost out there, but sometimes, if you get into a tangle you can smell and listen your way out. Seeing is only one way of getting to know the world around us.'

Thank you for your support of *Footsteps through the Fog*.

The author, Margaret Mahy, donated her royalties from the sale of this book to the Royal New Zealand Foundation of the Blind (RNZFB) and the illustrator Gavin Bishop has donated his time to illustrate it and bring the story to life. Sadly, Margaret passed away before this book was published.

Footsteps through the Fog is a story about Anthea, a child who is blind, and her adventures with her family on a foggy day. Anthea is just like every other child – she loves to play and to have days out at the beach.

The RNZFB helps blind and partially sighted children just like Anthea to play and to learn skills such as how to find their way to the park or use technology, and to do lots of other things that children do every day.

We hope you have enjoyed Anthea's story.

To find out more information about the RNZFB, please visit www.rnzfb.org.nz

Margaret Mahy

Margaret Mahy (1936–2012) was influential in changing the landscape of children's literature in her homeland.

She began writing children's books in earnest at the age of eighteen. In 1968 an American publisher came across the text of *A Lion in the Meadow* and bought it, along with all her other work.

Margaret Mahy became a full-time writer in 1980. Her novels *The Haunting* and *The Changeover* won the Carnegie Medal, and in 1986, she won the IBBY Honour Book Award.

In February 1993, Margaret was awarded New Zealand's highest honour, the Order of New Zealand. She also held an Honorary Doctorate of Letters from the University of Canterbury, New Zealand.

In 2006 she was awarded the Hans Christian Andersen Award, the highest international honour given to an author and an illustrator of children's books, in recognition of a lasting contribution to children's literature.

Gavin Bishop

Gavin Bishop (1946–) is a writer and illustrator of picture books whose timeless work ranges from Maori mythology to European fables and often features familiar New Zealand scenery and landmarks.

He has published some 50 children's books, which have been translated into nine languages. He has also written libretti for children's ballets for the Royal New Zealand Ballet and been a UNESCO guest author and speaker in Japan, China, Indonesia and the USA.

His awards are many – the New Zealand Children's Picture Book of the Year; the New Zealand Children's Book of the Year; and the Russell Clark Medal for Illustration; each won several times.

In 2000 he was awarded the Margaret Mahy Medal for Services to Children's Literature and in 2004 he was awarded the Sylvia Ashton-Warner Fellowship for Literacy. In 2009 the Storylines Gavin Bishop Award for New Illustrators was established in recognition of his work.